AF416994

LIFE IN A SNIPPET

A collection of nano-tales

LIFE IN A SNIPPET

A collection of nano-tales

ANJALI HINGER

HALF BAKED BEANS LITERATURE

e-mail:
publish.halfbakedbeans@gmail.
com First Published by Half
Baked Beans in 2021

Copyright © Anjali Hinger

All rights reserved. No part of this publication may be reproduced, stored in a retrieval system, or transmitted, in any form or by any means, electronic, mechanical photocopying, recording or otherwise, without the prior written permission bythe publisher.

Acknowledgement

For the wind beneath my wings:
my husband Gautam & daughter Rhea.

For my tower of strength:
my parents.

For my support system:
my family & family like friends.

Special thanks to my daughter Rhea for
designing the Cover Page of my book.

1.

Just when cynicism was on the brink of stepping in and her belief in love was about to wane, he came in her life and love bloomed once again.

2.

It took the newlyweds a lot of time to adjust to one another's habits, but while adjusting they unknowingly became each other's habit.

3.

Time has always been partial to her. It slows down when she is with him, and quickens its pace whenever they are apart.

4.

First fight; her brooding over their decision of marriage; him patching up by cooking a cheese Maggie dinner; dissipation of anxiety; love prevailing nonetheless.

5.

"The sea loves the sky more than the sky loves it." She said as they languorously watched the glorious dawn and the reflection of its pink-orange hues in the sea.

"Really?" He asked, bemused.

"Yes! See how the sea reflects every mood of the sky, just like someone who is utterly besotted and attuned to her beloved." She said, and entwining her fingers with his, she whispered to herself, "Someone like me."

6.

I always send a red heart emoji on her posts, not because I like them but to let her know that she matters.

7.

She freed her lips and glared with hatred, quelling my vain assumption that despite of brutally crushing her heart, my kiss could reignite her love.

8.

She loves my sense of humor, but doesn't know that I work exceedingly hard on it just to hear her tinkling laughter that tugs at my heartstrings in an unfathomable way.

9.

"Why do you wear the same dress every Friday and buy the same flowers?" The florist asked.

"We meet every Friday. He likes me in this dress and adores these wild flowers. Sorry, but I must rush now, he will be waiting." She said as she paid for the posy and hurried up the winding staircase which led to the cemetery where he lay buried.

10.

She was the most imprudent and infuriating girl that he had ever met, but also the only one who made his heart skip a beat.

11.

It was their first gay parade together. As he clasped his partner's fingers tightly, he saw him flash a loving smile and thought how he had almost abandoned his true love to escape the wrath of the society.

12.

He reveled in his love for her; it was real, steady and magical. But there was just one little hitch in the love story...he still had to confess his feelings to her.

13.

Seeing him again brought back several happy memories, and she ran towards him to embrace him but stopped midway as she remembered with a jolt that she was somebody else's wife now.

14.

It was her absence that made him realize how much her presence meant to him.

15.

It so happened one day, that my reason lost its way and reluctantly allowed love to lead. Reckless love took the forbidden path and gushed through my un-trodden, shriveled heart, plumped it awake, and evoked all the dormant emotions in its wake.

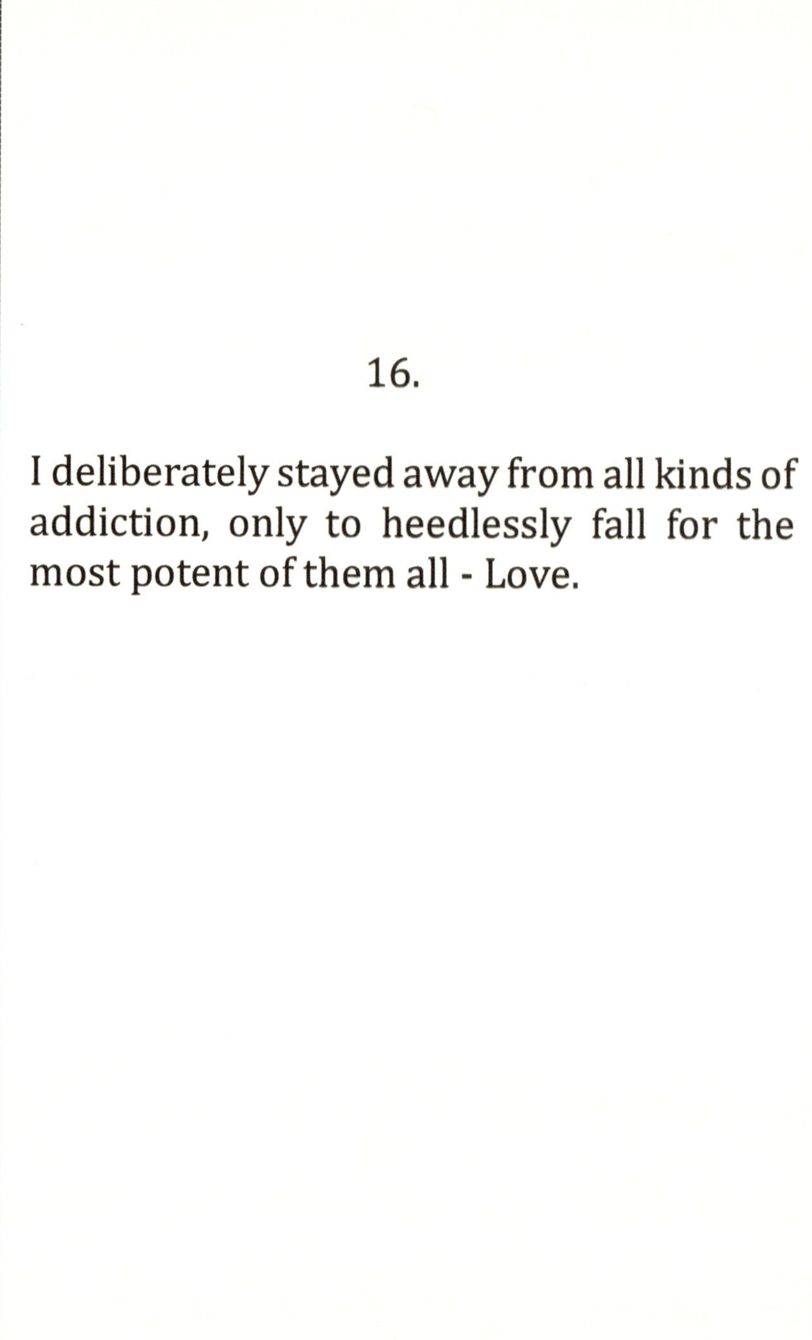

16.

I deliberately stayed away from all kinds of addiction, only to heedlessly fall for the most potent of them all - Love.

17.

"I tried not to fall in love with you, but in vain." She said slowly.

"I know the feeling, because I too, have been futilely trying to un-love you from the past few years." He said after a long pause, the carefully hidden emotions now evident in his eyes.

18.

"I can decipher that he loves her by the way he looks at her." She paused before adding slowly, "And I know that look pretty well, because that is how I look at him."

19.

He wooed her with everything that a woman could possibly dream of, but eventually realized that hearts are won, not bought.

20.

18 years- My best friend gifted me a dainty gold filigree heart pendant from his first salary.

40 years- We gifted that pendant to our daughter on her 18th birthday.

21.

The obscenely expensive engagement ring on my finger was fetching a lot of envious glances, but my heart was yearning to swap it with the plain silver band that my true love had given me.

22.

Our waning love could have bloomed despite the differences, but his fragile ego and my broken trust conspired and ensured that we couldn't unite again.

23.

I had deliberately sealed all the passages to my heart, but this utterly annoying slip of a girl somehow managed to dance her way in, and much to my dismay, just refuses to leave now and constantly creates havoc inside by accelerating my heartbeats and tugging at my heartstrings every time she looks and smiles at me.

24.

The orange painted lips have a story to tell. That bold colour had triggered an instant attraction between them, but he broke up with her after a while. Since then, she has been colouring her lips orange every day, in hope that it will lure him back to her.

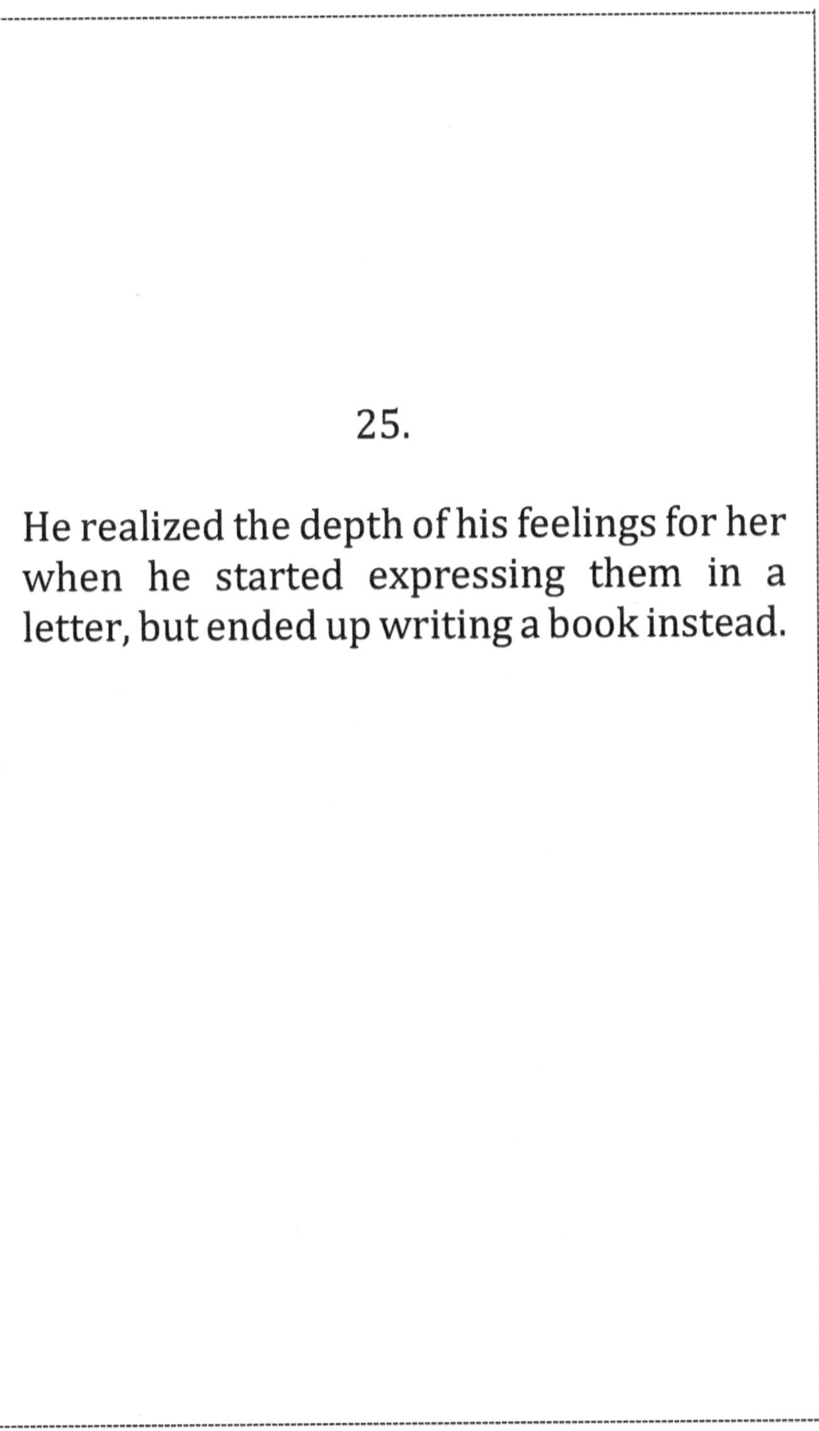

25.

He realized the depth of his feelings for her when he started expressing them in a letter, but ended up writing a book instead.

26.

The whiff of her scent lingers in my senses and energizes me to finish my work like a maniac, so that I can rush back to her domain to inhale that vanilla flavored air which is keeping me alive these days.

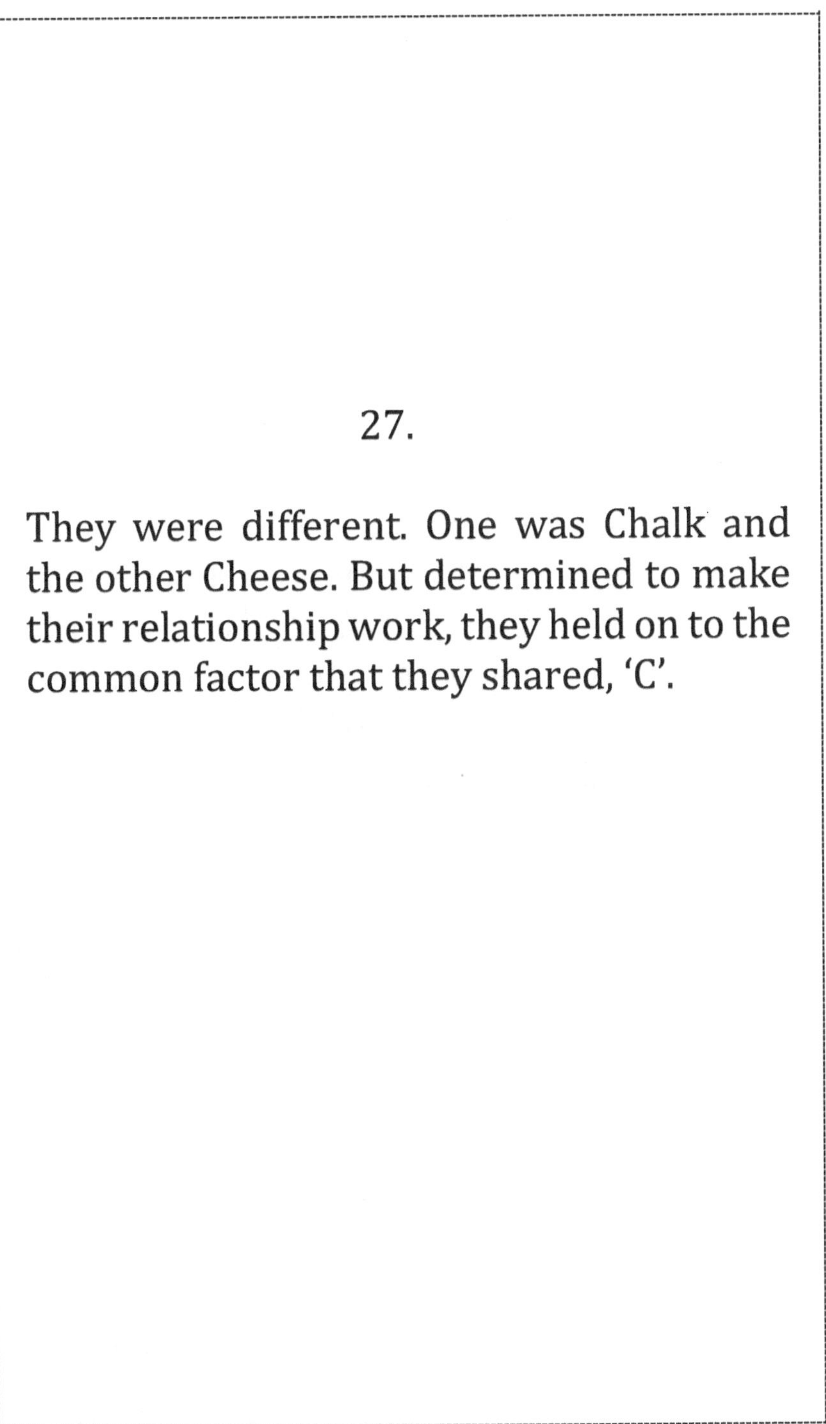

27.

They were different. One was Chalk and the other Cheese. But determined to make their relationship work, they held on to the common factor that they shared, 'C'.

28.

The reasons to leave him are enough to fill Pandora's box, but whenever I try to break up with him, his irresistible 'sorry' smile somehow manages to cloud my logic, and compels me to give him a second, a third and a fourth chance.

29.

"Mmm! Can there be a better sweet and sour combination than this?" She asked, as they devoured the scrumptious sweet and sour stir fry noodles. "Yes! Spending the rest of our lives together." He answered, without blinking his eyes.

30.

She broke her stiletto heel and was sitting barefoot at the office party, feeling miserably awkward. He sat down beside her, opened his shoes and said casually, "It is too hot to wear shoes, isn't it?" They smiled at each other and cupid struck.

31.

She subconsciously wore colours that reflected her mood. Yesterday, dressed in a bright red, she had picked up a fight with him for a trifle, but she might patch up today, he decoded as he saw her entering the office in a fetching white dress. He quickly hid a knowing grin as she stopped by his desk and offered him a sweet smile with a cup of steaming hot coffee.

32.

Her pursuit of finding love left a failed marriage and three bitter affairs in its wake. And when she finally gave up, thinking that it was just not destined...love found her.

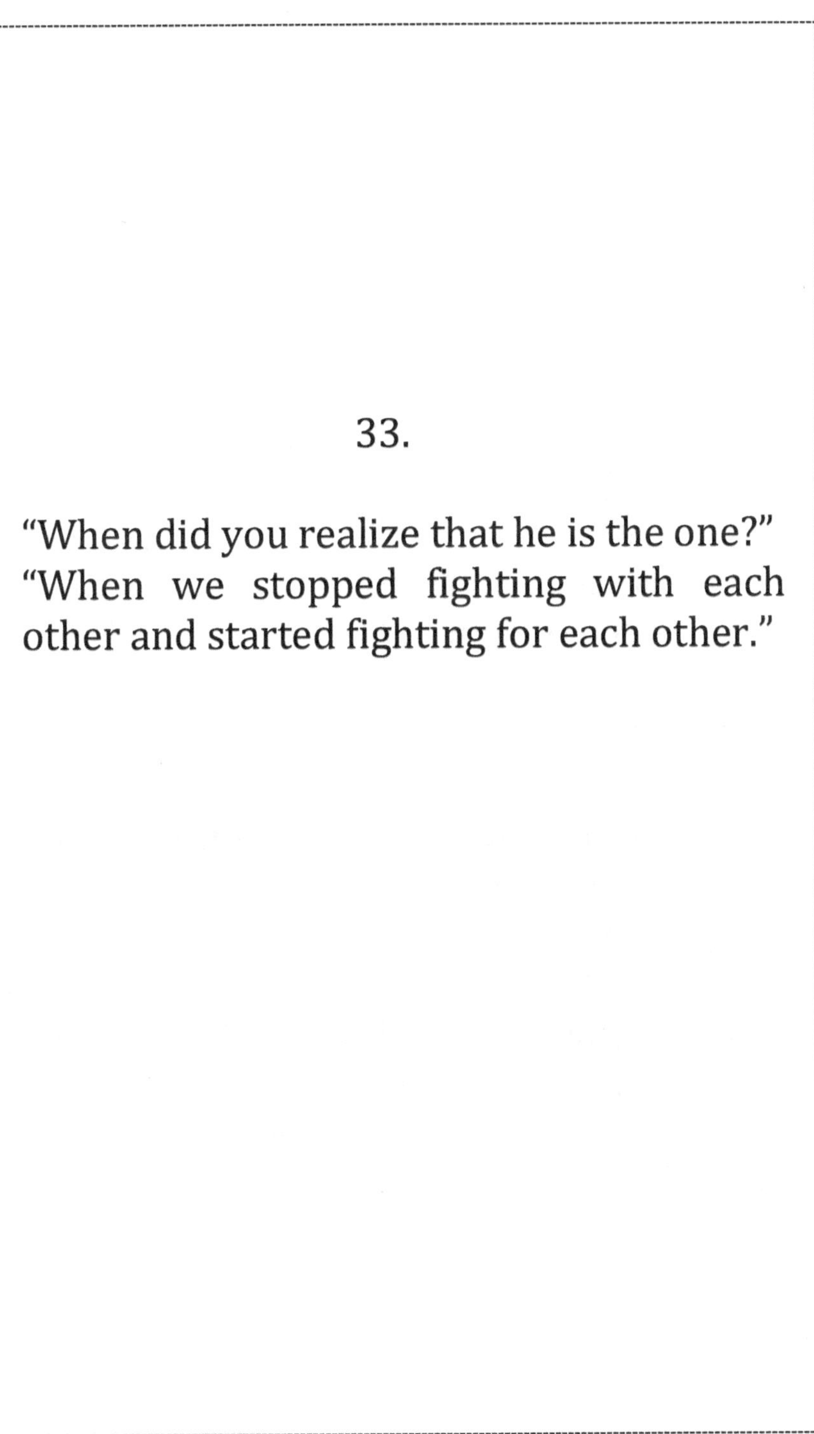

33.

"When did you realize that he is the one?"
"When we stopped fighting with each other and started fighting for each other."

34.

"Happy new year, my love!" Getting down on one knee, he opened a ring box and popped the question.

"Will you be mine for this year?"

"Yes, my darling! I was hoping for this." She answered ecstatically and flung her arms around him. 'Forever' had been redefined and had acquired a flexible span, that changed according to honest commitments.

35.

There was nothing particularly special about her, but her smile penetrated my stone-cold heart and the ice inside started melting. Caution and reason bubbled up but I ignored their reprimands and decided to go with my gut instinct, just for once.

36.

"How can you bear to leave your home, this lavish mansion where you have spent your entire life for his tiny apartment in a dingy lane?" They asked. She smiled and answered simply, "Home is where the heart is, and my heart has a new address now."

37.

"Love has beautiful hues especially when it comes with freedom. Fear gets replaced by self-dignity, prejudice wanes and leaves behind a feeling of complete bliss." An ecstatic man said to his gay partner as they walked hand in hand freely for the first time. "And yes, only clothes go in the closet from now on." He added with a smile.

38.

She sobbed, expecting rejection. But dismissing her disfigured leg, he embraced her thinking of his scarred and broken heart which only she could heal.

39.

"You are like that shiny kite, a blend of beauty and success soaring high in the sky, but sometimes I feel that your husband holds the string and tugs you down whenever he feels that you are flying higher than him." Someone said to her.

"Yes, he tugs, but only to keep me away from the obstructions that can waver my flight." She said with a smile.

40.

She cared for him, understood him and was his best friend, but the only problem was that they always had a crush on the same guy.

41.

Star gazing was just an excuse to steal some glances at her as he couldn't muster the courage to approach her. She broke the ice one day, and now they hold hands and frequently exchange loving looks while watching the stars, and their eyes twinkle brighter than them.

42.

Our story couldn't be completed, but it still occupies the same place in my heart.

43.

They fought, broke up and she left his house in a fit of anger. As she sat in the car, her phone beeped, "Drive safe and text once you reach."

44.

When the whole world is practicing social distancing and self-isolation, some long lost relationships are rekindling on social networking sites.

45.

The filters made her look absolutely stunning, but she opted to upload her original picture on the matrimonial site. After all, a new relationship should never start on a false note.

46.

Some quintessential days somehow manage to leave a mark in your life, especially when you somehow manage to ram your new scooter into a sports car, whose angry rude owner somehow manages to fall for you, and somehow manages to woo you to become his life partner.

Sometimes, such days are just destined to be.

47.

A shiver ran down her spine at the sight of the red rose.

"Red reminds me of my abusive and traumatic past." She said shakily.

"From now on, it will remind you only of my love." He said, and pressing the rose in her hand, he covered her palm gently but firmly with his own.

48.

The letter of his martyrdom reached a decade late, and the thick wall of bitterness, that was built on the deceptive portrayal of his betrayal, came crumbling down with her tears of sorrow.

49.

He climbed mountains, the steepest and the sloppiest.

"Why?" She asked.

"It gives me a high to conquer the unattainable, untamed." He said.

"Is that why you married me?" She asked lightly, releasing her hair from the confinement of her racing helmet, and letting the unruly florescent pink streaked curls bounce on her shoulders.

50.

"Missing you both!" Husband, daughter and I said to each other on the video chat.

"Don't worry, we shall be together soon." I said, teary eyed.

No, we are not living in three different continents, just three different rooms of our house...separated by Corona.

51.

Her blue Pashmina shawl was painstakingly mended at several places. The colour had faded from cornflower blue to a grey variant. It was a mismatch with her upscale clothes and jewellery, but it was a fixture. People were amused by her obsession but she didn't care. And only I knew that my mother had been donning it every day since the last 15 years, because she felt my father's presence and love in that shawl which had been his last gift to her.

52.

"How did this placid, docile woman turn into a fierce warrior?"

"Somebody provoked the mother in her."

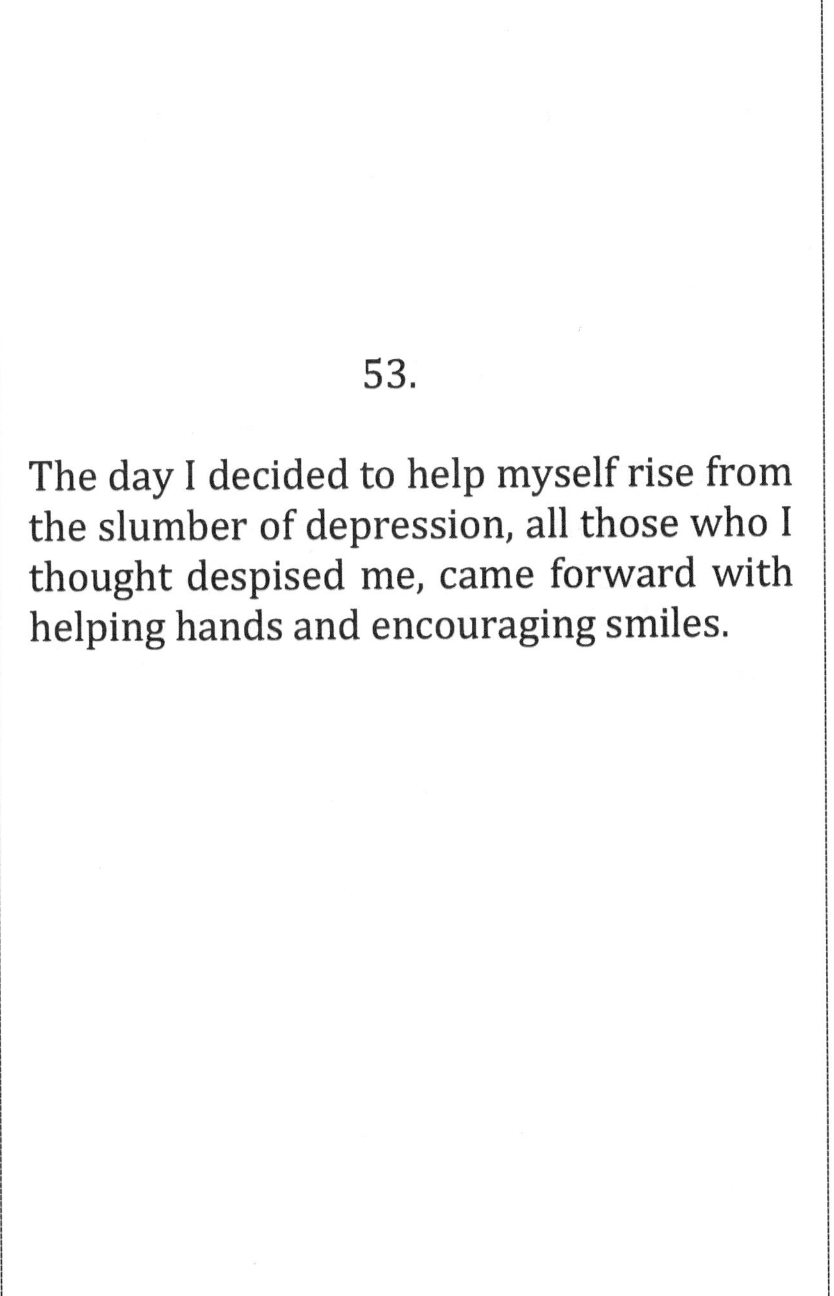

53.

The day I decided to help myself rise from the slumber of depression, all those who I thought despised me, came forward with helping hands and encouraging smiles.

54.

The bride's calm smile was a stark juxtaposition to the anguish storming inside her, the anguish of being forced to betray her true love for pseudo-family-honor.

55.

When tea was served in cheap opaque glasses amid mindless wordplay of friends, I longed for refined solitude.

And now, when tea is served in the finest bone china with freshly baked almond biscottis, the heart yearns for that senseless banter.

56.

They called him a recluse. "Little do they know, I socialize more than they do." He said, "I spend hours mingling with my best friends: my pen, notepad, plants and my precious pipe."

57.

We bonded like we had been welded together as one, but now it is a threesome, and the uninvited, intruding huge void sits between us all the time.

58.

I swallowed the lump in my throat and pushed the sleeping pills back into the bottle. My son's "Ma, I love you." had meddled with my decision of giving up, compelling the mother in me to live and fight.

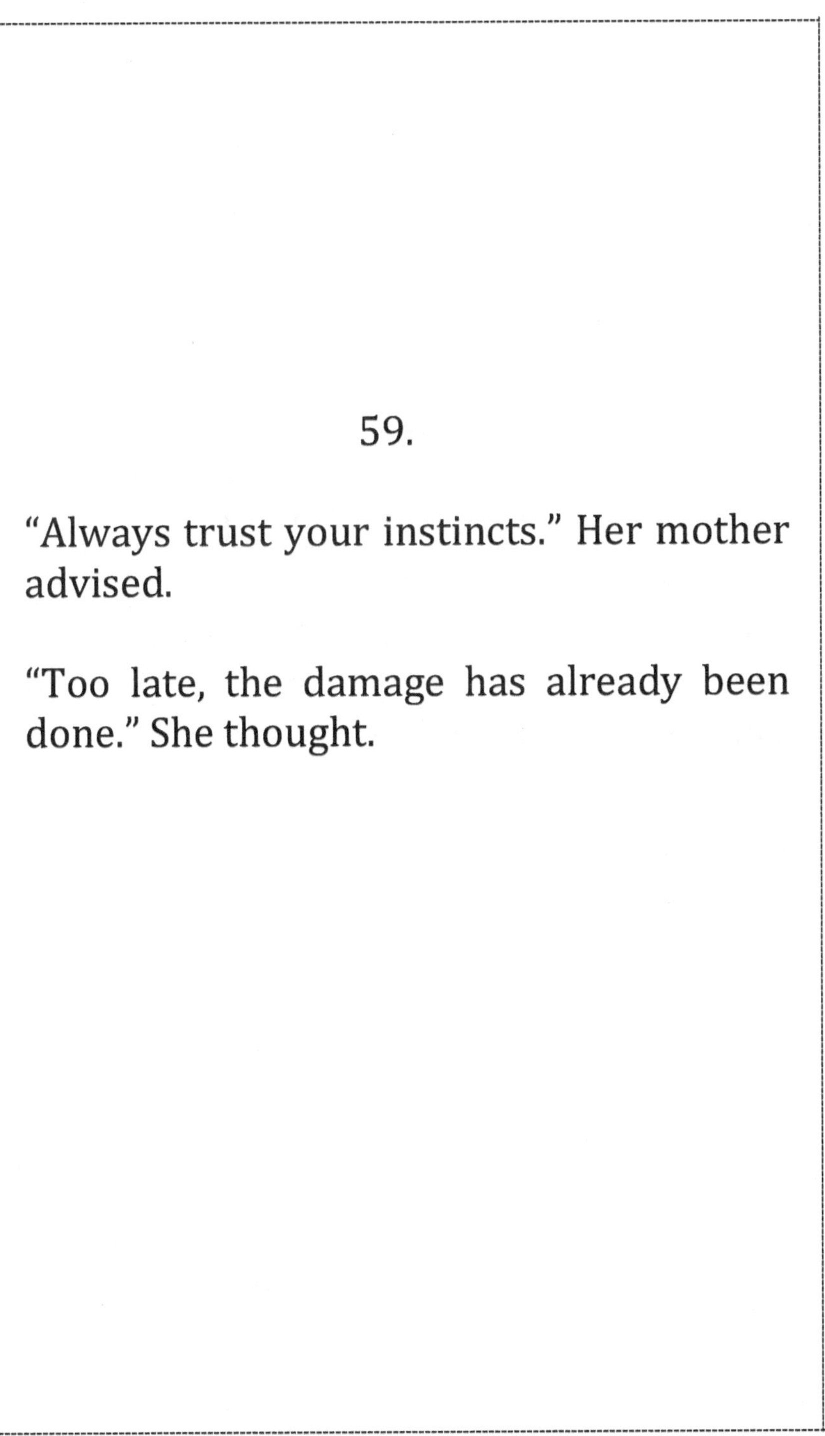

59.

"Always trust your instincts." Her mother advised.

"Too late, the damage has already been done." She thought.

60.

I have never looked better. With a satisfied smile, I deepen the red lipstick and slip my feet into matching stilettos. "Why are you wearing mom's things, bro?" A baffled voice asks from behind.

61.

"All well, honey?"

"Absolutely."

"No, something is bothering you."

"How do you always find out?"

"A - Because you tend to binge on chocolates when you are perturbed, just like you are doing right now; and B-Because I am your mother." Maa said tenderly and ruffled my hair.

62.

She realized that she had failed to convince her best friend about her dinner date, when she found a tiny pepper spray in her clutch bag with a note stuck on it that said, "He might be decent, but a best friend's gotta do what a best friend's gotta do."

63.

"Botox may iron the creases of my face, but will it smoothen the wrinkles of my poor heart that increase multifold whenever you go on your expeditions?" A mountaineer's mother asked him when he offered her a makeover for her birthday.

64.

My customarily peaceful and spotless house is pulsating with blaring music and is strewn with clothes, dirty plates, half eaten pizzas and scattered DVDs. But today, even a hyper fastidious person like me is loving it. After all, it is not every day that my children come home for their summer vacation.

65.

As they stepped inside the school for their reunion meet, the bunch of sophisticated ladies transformed into chirpy and carefree girls, and years just melted away.

66.

My doting parents left no stone unturned in making me feel like a princess on my birthday, and I didn't have the heart to tell them that I had more fun cutting a little out of shape and stale pastry amidst my hostel friends, than the designer cake that they had lovingly brought for me.

67.

Her rebel and reckless streak, which had once got her labeled as the black sheep of the family, has now made her an international racing driver, and needless to say... the star of her family.

68.

The pink faded lounge chair looked radically out of place in that snazzy leather and chrome bachelor's pad. But it had been his mother's favorite, and was the only thing in the house that made it a home!

69.

"You don't trust me enough."

"Well, if you have trust issues, then don't ever talk to me again." Stomping their feet, the best friends glared at each other in the lunch break and parted ways. The evening saw them huddled up in a corner of a cafe, discussing animatedly about a boy in their class...the little spat forgotten completely.

70.

I contemplated suicide many a time, but each time, the balming effect of my mom's unconditional love, soothed the blisters erupted by my defeats.

71.

He had a myopic attitude towards women and she was a liberated soul. Their parents got them married and they lived happily ever after... after their divorce, of course.

72.

The military base had one more martyr's photograph on the wall now, and the entire regiment had one more invisible wound in their hearts.

73.

Scooping her up in a huge bear hug, Santa twirled her around and said, "Merry Christmas, muffin." His voice was husky with emotions because he, the duty bound army officer was seeing her after two long years. Surprised and overwhelmed, she hugged him back tightly and said, "Merry Christmas! I missed you so much daddy." Her Santa turned out to be her best Christmas gift ever.

74.

Drenched by unexpected showers, I landed at her doorstep by chance...to be greeted by a charming smile, a concerned look, aroma of masala chai, soothing strains of sitar and a warm fluffy towel, and I instantly knew that I was home.

75.

What keeps you going on the cold, lonely nights?" I happened to ask a soldier posted on a frozen mountain.

"The fact that my daughter is sleeping safely in her bed warms my heart and melts all the ice around me." He answered with a smile.

Courage has a face.

76.

"Why do they inject baby vegetables?" A five-years old asked his parents.

"Chemicals plump up vegetables promptly which increases sales and saves time, but it also makes veggies toxic so we should always let nature run its course." The father said, adding, "Now run along, don't you have your piano class followed by French and karate classes?"

"In a way, aren't we doing the same to our child?" His mother wondered.

77.

Her mom refused to let her attend a late night party. She slammed the door angrily and went to bed without having dinner. Though she never came to know, but two people had slept hungry that night.

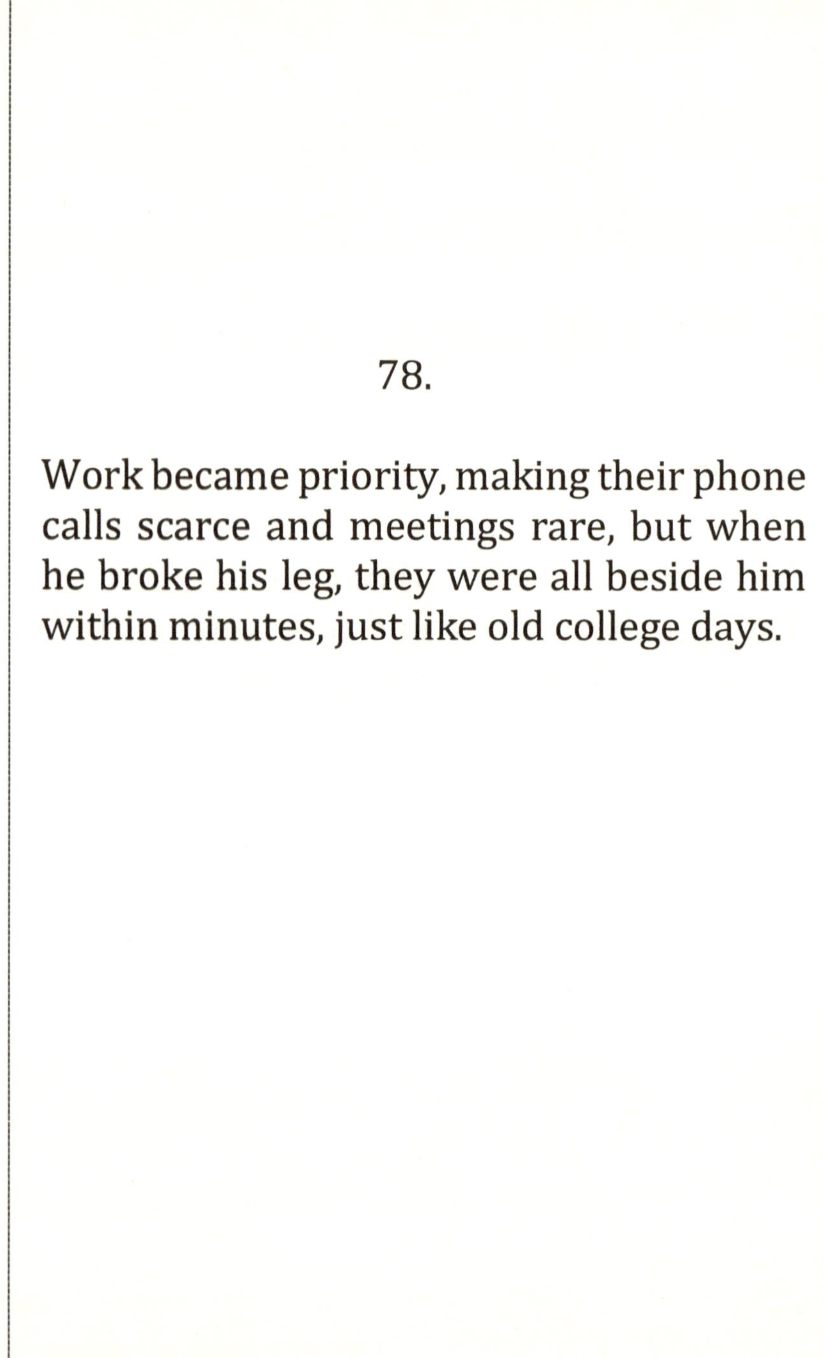

78.

Work became priority, making their phone calls scarce and meetings rare, but when he broke his leg, they were all beside him within minutes, just like old college days.

79.

As she touched the indented ring mark on her now ring-less finger, a relieved smile of being able to breathe freely again spread on her face, because the suffocating patriarchy that had come with the ornate ring had left her gasping for fresh air.

80.

Hear my side of the story too before judging who is responsible for our breakup, because just being frail and teary eyed does not qualify her of not being guilty.

81.

She blamed him for her own infidelity as it was much easier than claiming responsibility for it, but guilt supported him by clinging to her and nagging her whenever it got a chance.

82.

Ignoring social pressure, the newlyweds filed for a mutual divorce, because rather than being miserable together, it was better to stay happy apart.

83.

The gleaming ring was burning a hole in his pocket but he was waiting for the right time to propose, and it was only when he saw someone else's ring on her finger that he realized that you can either keep waiting for the right time or you can make the time right.

84.

Convinced by his intellect that he was emotionally damaged beyond repair, he grudgingly gave his heart a chance and was led into a sublime ocean of love that healed him completely.

85.

"Feeling bored, he took a rose from a vase, crushed it ruthlessly and threw the debris on the ground.

"You did the same to me, and transformed a buoyant girl into a doormat wife." She whispered sadly as she bent down to collect the remains of the exquisite flower.

86.

When the vacuum in her heart became unbearable, she embraced it and made it her comfort zone.

87.

He could have dealt with her hatred, it was her indifference that shattered him.

88.

Her lips were always sealed, but her expressive brown eyes betrayed her each time and conveyed her agony more explicitly than any words could.

89.

He knew their relationship was over, when he called her and heard an impassive, "Wrong number!" in her voice followed by the disconnect tone.

90.

And the rain cringed clouds reflected the state of my heart, there were no tears left now...only a void.

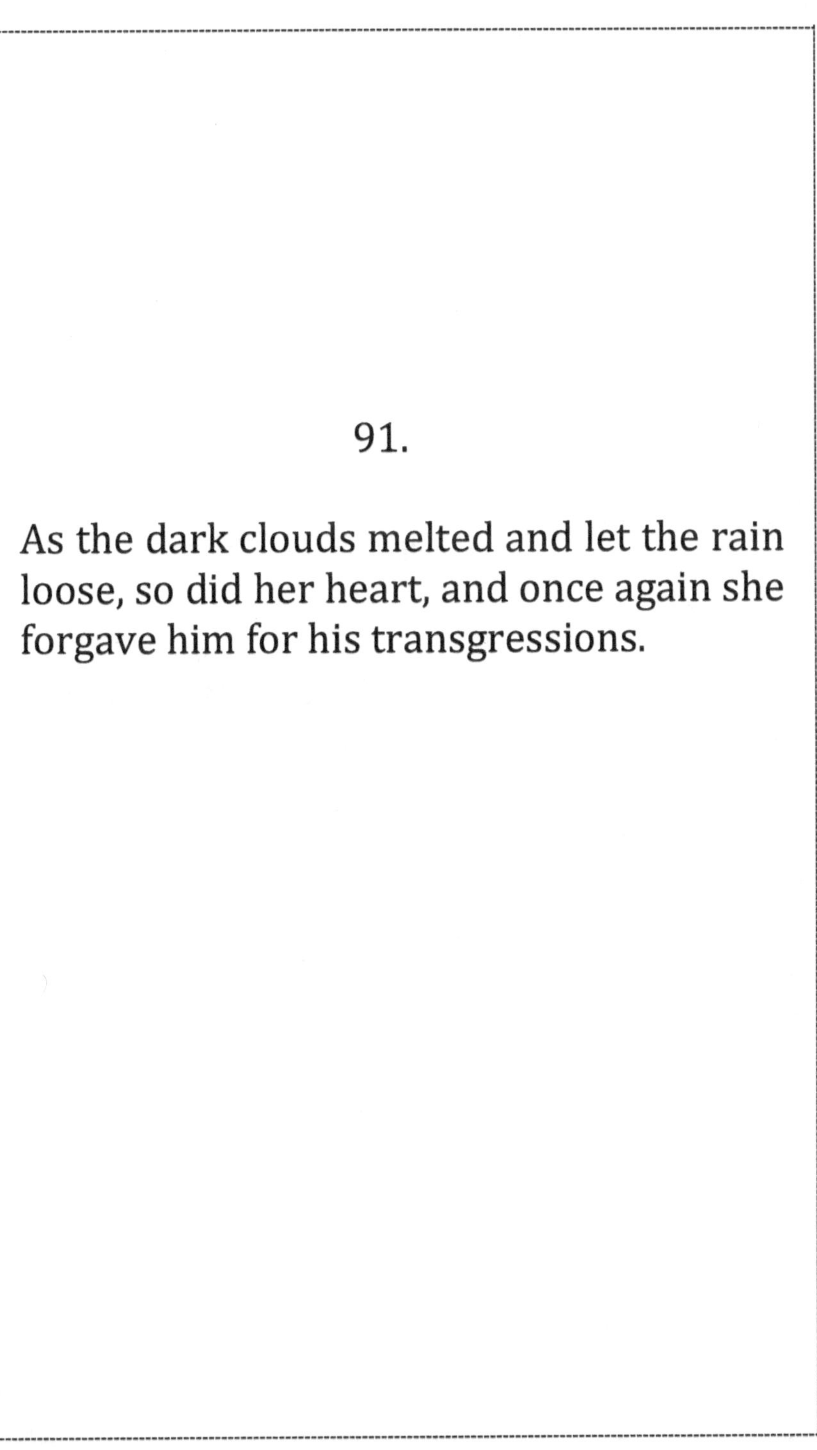

91.

As the dark clouds melted and let the rain loose, so did her heart, and once again she forgave him for his transgressions.

92.

The winds of change changed a lot of things.

Some saw it as a catastrophe, while some saw it as a new beginning.

93.

She dumped me, crushed my self-esteem and drove me to depression, but still, she was the only reason I didn't give up on life. Nah, she didn't start reciprocating my feelings again, but because I couldn't be a loser in her eyes.

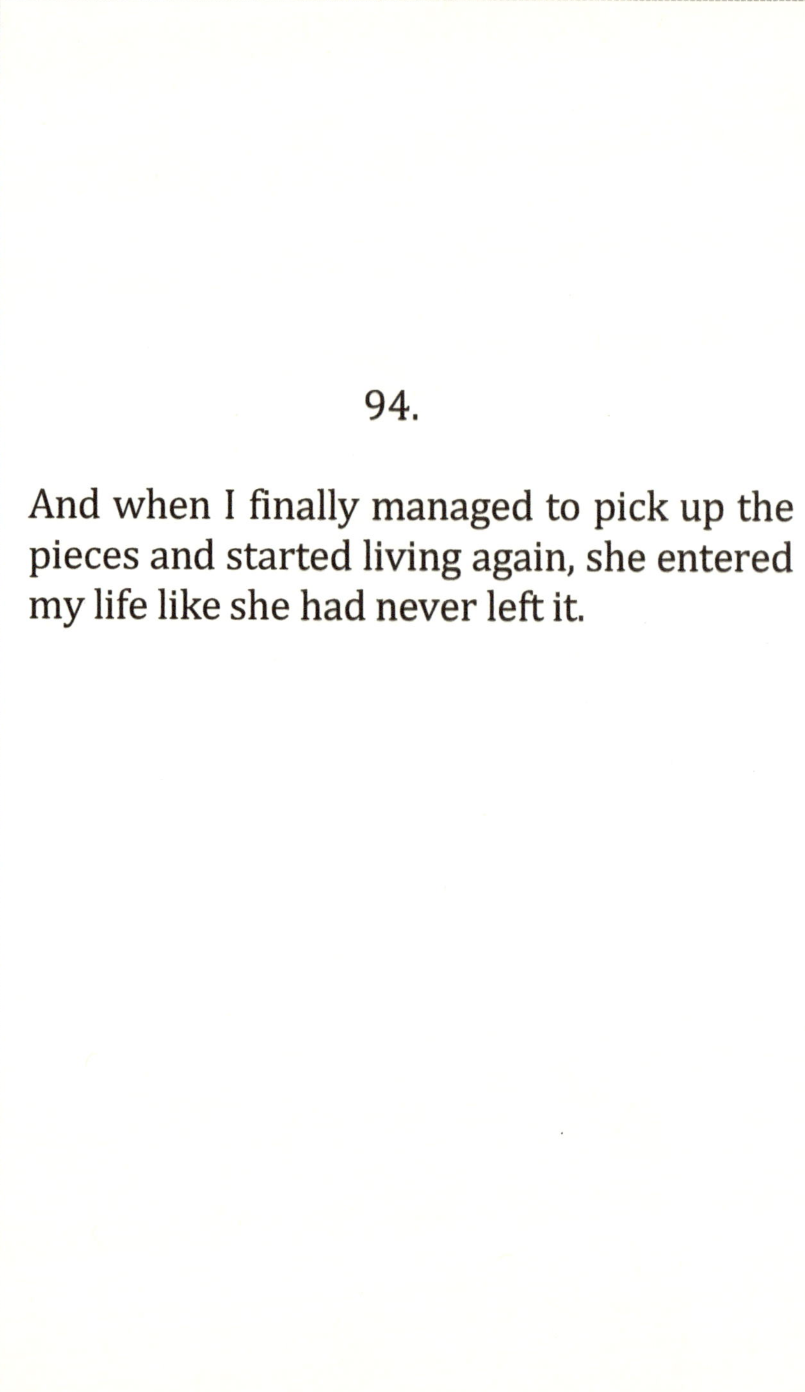

94.

And when I finally managed to pick up the pieces and started living again, she entered my life like she had never left it.

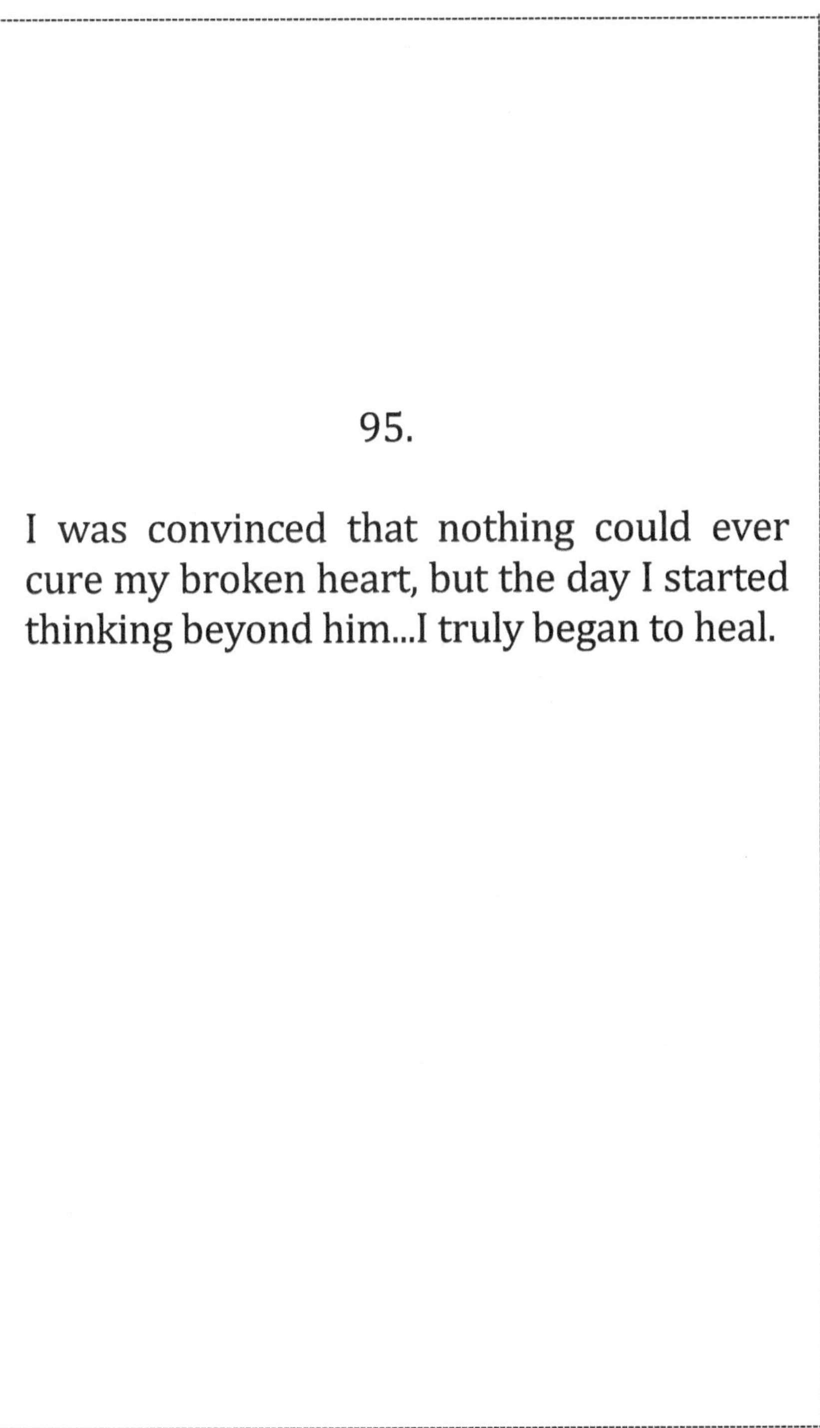

95.

I was convinced that nothing could ever cure my broken heart, but the day I started thinking beyond him...I truly began to heal.

96.

Many things have changed in these past few years, but some things have been constant, like my love for you and your indifference towards me.

97.

"Was your love for real?"

"Hmm... the deep crevices in my heart are a testament to it."

98.

She was her usual self once again: cheerful, radiant and high on life.

All it took was a break-up.

99.

A powerful voice against body shaming, he always emphasized that real beauty lies within, but secretly wished to marry a fair, slim and beautiful girl.

100.

I don't know what affected me more - his treason or my naiveté for falling for a traitor.

101.

I had trustingly handed my much-guarded heart to her, which she ruthlessly tossed aside once her purpose was served, leaving it vulnerable and tainted.

102.

Dating her was a fantasy,
that became a misjudged reality,
and is now a distressing memory.

103.

"Don't feel insecure; my success just proves that you are not god and that both of us are mortals, not just me." She said to her dominating and prejudiced husband, her newly found confidence glinting in her eyes.

104.

So very engrossed was the successful marriage counselor in mending others' broken marital relationships that she didn't even realize that her own marriage was slowly falling apart.

105.

They blamed him for her heartbreak and called him an infidel, but the truth was that he was the one nursing a bruised heart ever since she had left him for somebody else. But, his heart still beat for her, and so, as usual...he was still covering up for her.

106.

When they were strangers, she was totally smitten with him.

And now, she wants them to become strangers again.

107.

She gatecrashed my colourless mundane life and blobbed it with bright colours, spread laughter all around, changed my cynical mindset and taught me how to live. And when I started living for the first time in my life...she left me as simply as an autumn leaf would fall off a tree.

108.

Last night, he had spiked her drink and his actions had spiked her love for him, liberally with vengeance. Tonight, wearing a short dress and a pasted smile on her face, she fingered the shiny knife hidden in her clutch before knocking at his door, determined to show him the consequence of betraying a best friend's trust.

109.

She was sipping tea, oblivious to the chaos caused in the wake of a bomb explosion near her office. After her catastrophic divorce, even the bomb blasts were sounding soothing.

110.

"Did she commit suicide?" They asked when her body was found floating in a lake along with a capsized boat.

"No." He said in a broken voice, "The boat couldn't balance the weight of her miseries."

111.

"So, we can say that these ruins are a result of hatred and rancour." The history teacher said, concluding the story of an ancient ravaged castle. And for a moment there, I thought he was talking about my heart.

112.

He was a dominating narcissist while she lusted for freedom. His pride couldn't take a simple no, and she finally got her wings.

113.

Odd, but she could feel the loud music resonating her loneliness.

And it dawned on her that being an escapist and partying endlessly would never heal her broken heart, only facing the music and moving on would.

114.

That one denial took away my marriage, the mansion, credit cards, cars and the heirloom jewels, but in my new, cramped one room apartment, I found the most precious things that I had lost: my self-respect, dignity, peace of mind and happiness.

115.

He walked out of the court, a free man. His eyes were twinkling with joy and there was a spring in his step. "But your guilt will keep you chained forever." A voice whispered from behind. Shocked, he turned around and found his conscience confronting him.

116.

Instead of being a part of a predefined story where she could gaze at the sky, she decided to write her own wherein she'd rather touch the sky.

117.

She drank in the tranquility of the sea and let it absorb her inner unruly storm of carefully hidden emotions, much fiercer than these waters had ever seen.

118.

Pandemic wasn't so bad for her because she could drop the pretense and be what she actually was: socially awkward!

119.

A few days in the quiet sanctity of the wilderness made her realize that there was much more to life than being a part of the mayhem of the concrete jungle.

120.

She watched the beautiful red and gold gondola tied on the edge of the river, and thought how it echoed her life. It could sway from side to side, but moved only when the boatman wanted.

121.

She stores all the beautiful moments like extra sugar cubes, ready to mix whenever life's sweet quotient goes down.

122.

A curveball can turn your life upside down, but my topsy-turvy life needed a curveball to set it straight.

123.

Doors, I believe are fascinating story tellers. They stir your imagination to brew stories about secrets that lie behind closed doors, and make you live different stories, once you open them and step inside.

124.

He opted for the less travelled, perilously winding road, as it had lesser bends than the twisted brains that he had been dealing with.

125.

Depressed due to his failures, he was startled one day, when hope backslapped him and said cheerfully, "Let's get going, buddy."

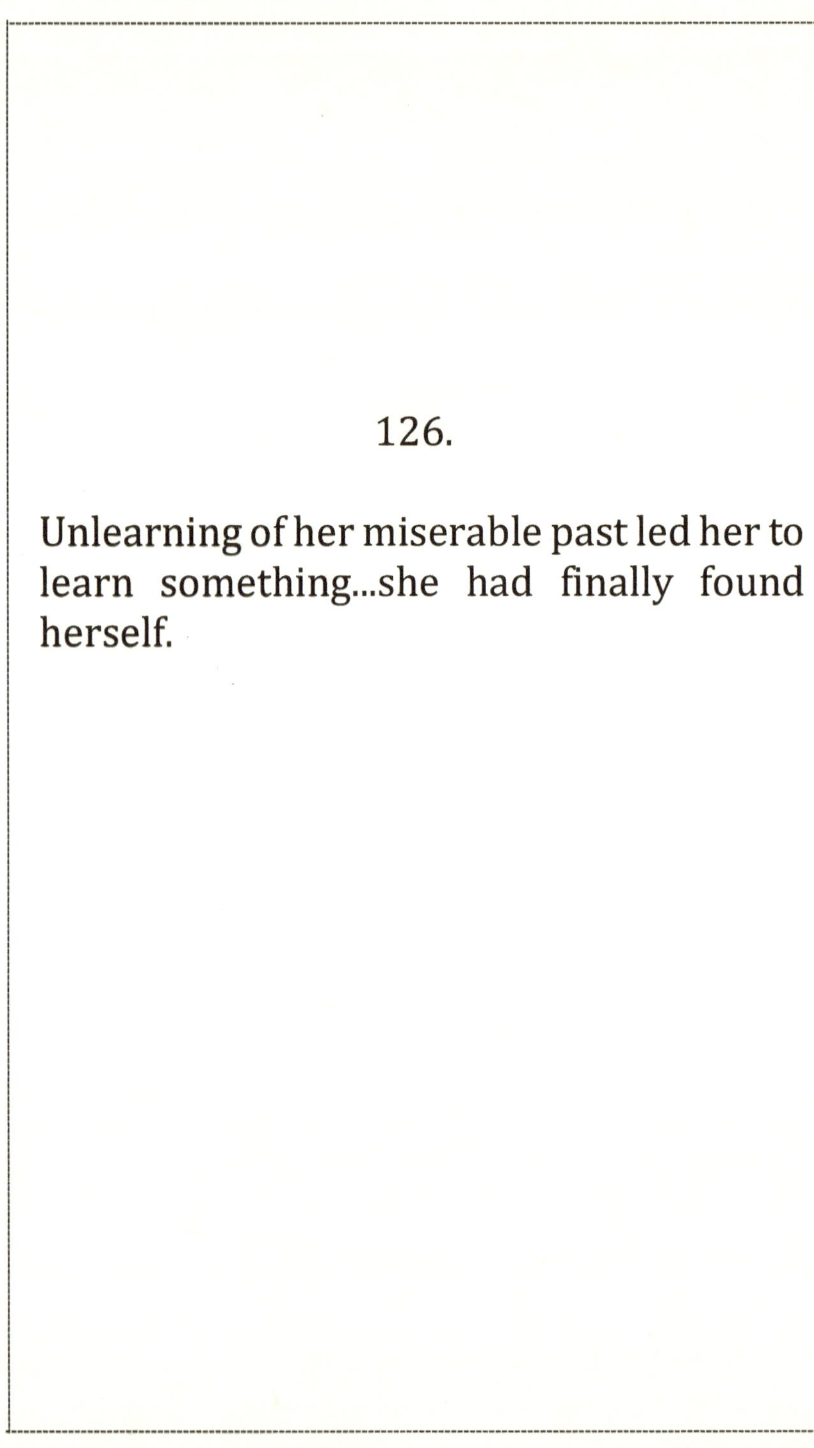

126.

Unlearning of her miserable past led her to learn something...she had finally found herself.

127.

"Optimism is as contagious as a viral disease. You either infect people or you impact people."

128.

Some days, I escape the confines of the clouds and gasp admiringly at my own reflection in the water.

"No wonder everybody is in awe of my beauty." I think with pride.

"No, No! I am not a narcissist, but I just can't help being dazzled by every avatar of mine."

I, the moon clarify my stance.

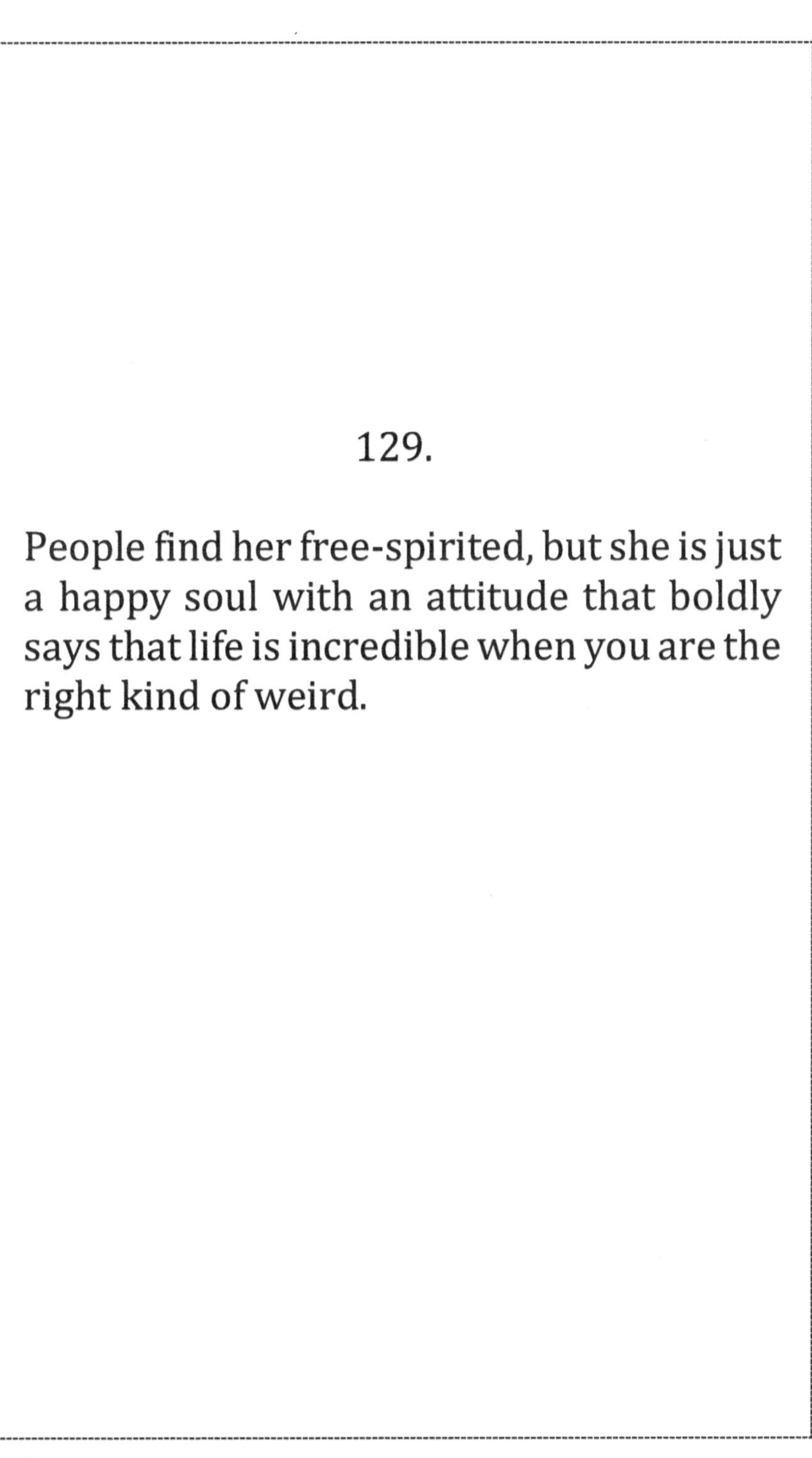

129.

People find her free-spirited, but she is just a happy soul with an attitude that boldly says that life is incredible when you are the right kind of weird.

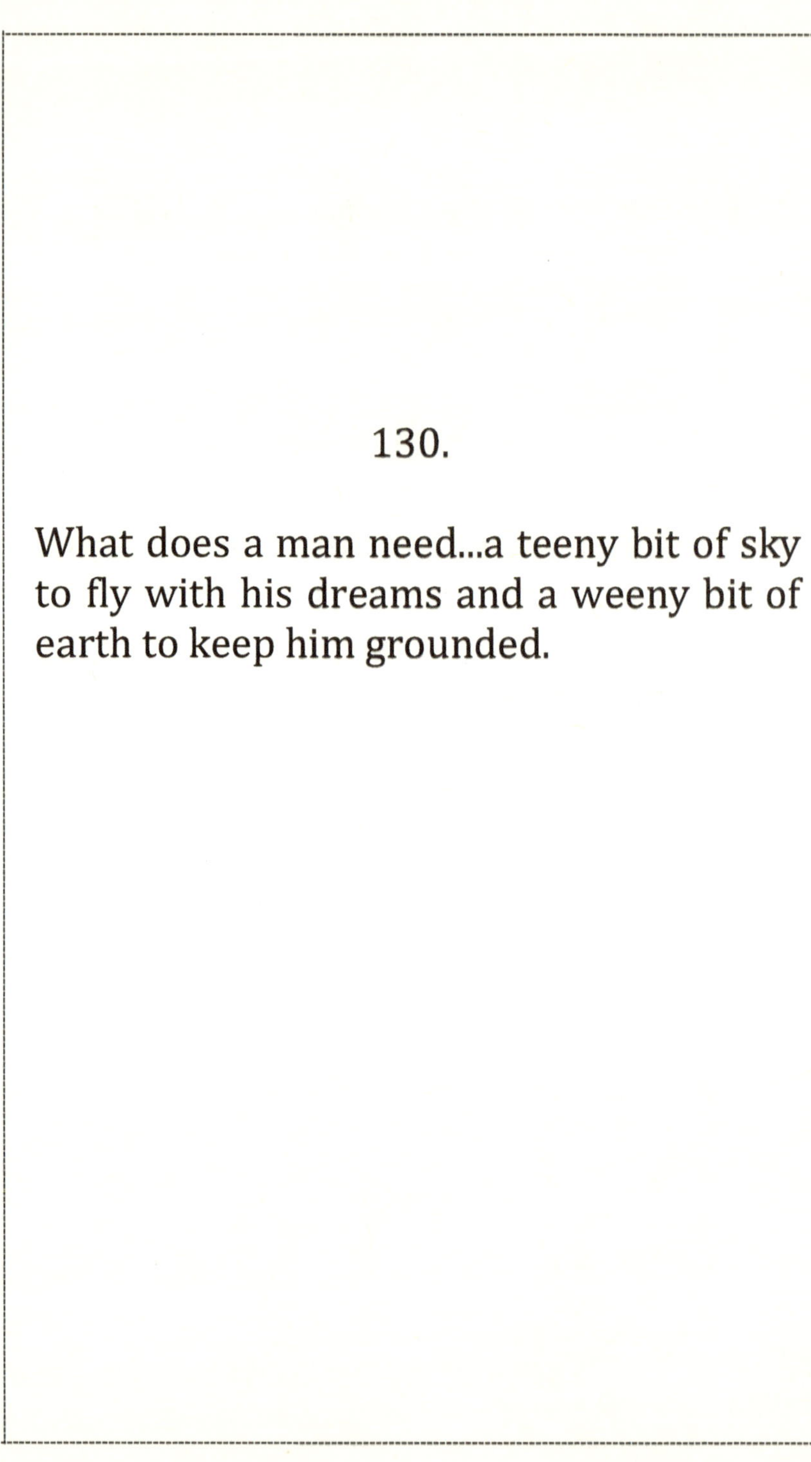

130.

What does a man need...a teeny bit of sky to fly with his dreams and a weeny bit of earth to keep him grounded.

131.

You complained because you chose to see only thorns in the rose bushes, while she rejoiced because she saw roses blooming in thorn bushes. The world is alike for everybody, but how you perceive it makes all the difference.

132.

People told her that a new day was all she needed to start over, but she realized that it was a new mindset that mattered... irrespective of the day.

133.

Too awkward to fit in, he decided to stand out... and made a mark.

134.

The grass, as always, was looking greener on the other side, but she figured out that it just took a strong will and a pair of sturdy shoes to get there.

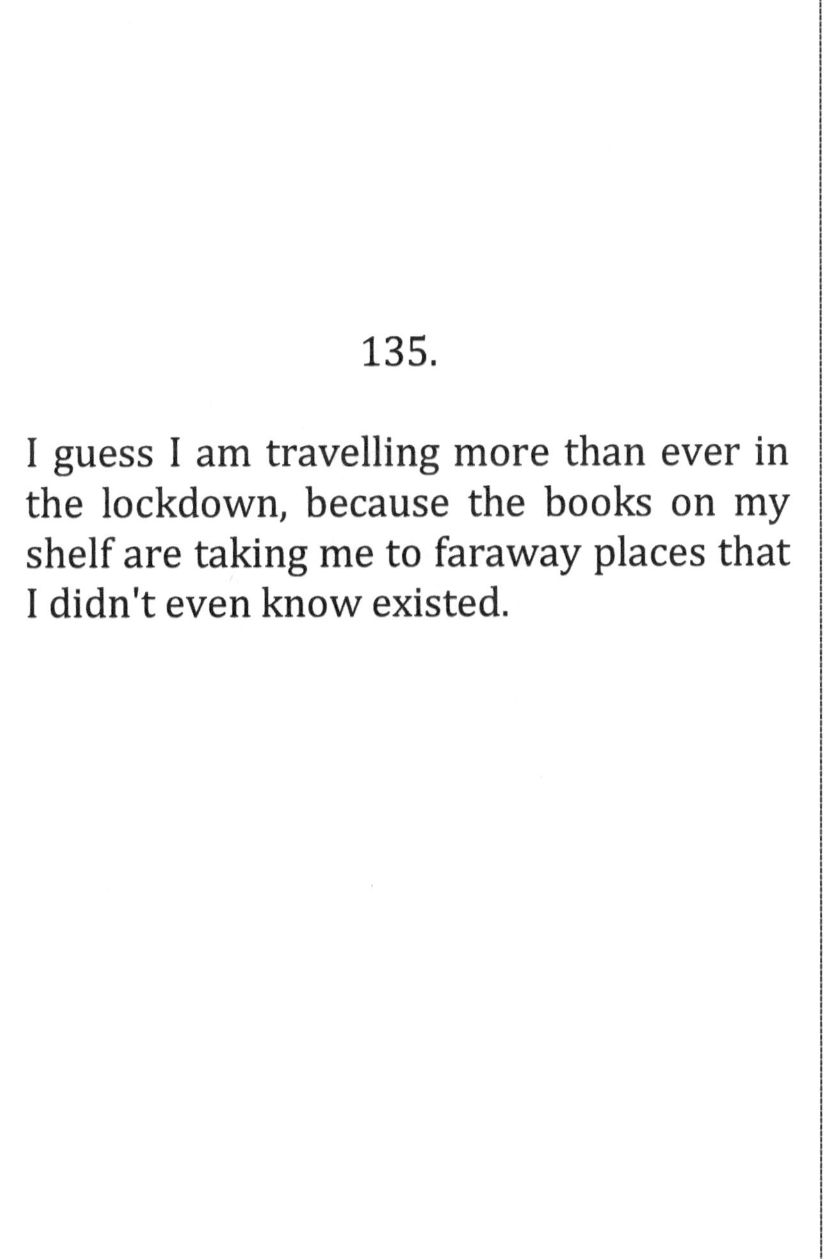

135.

I guess I am travelling more than ever in the lockdown, because the books on my shelf are taking me to faraway places that I didn't even know existed.

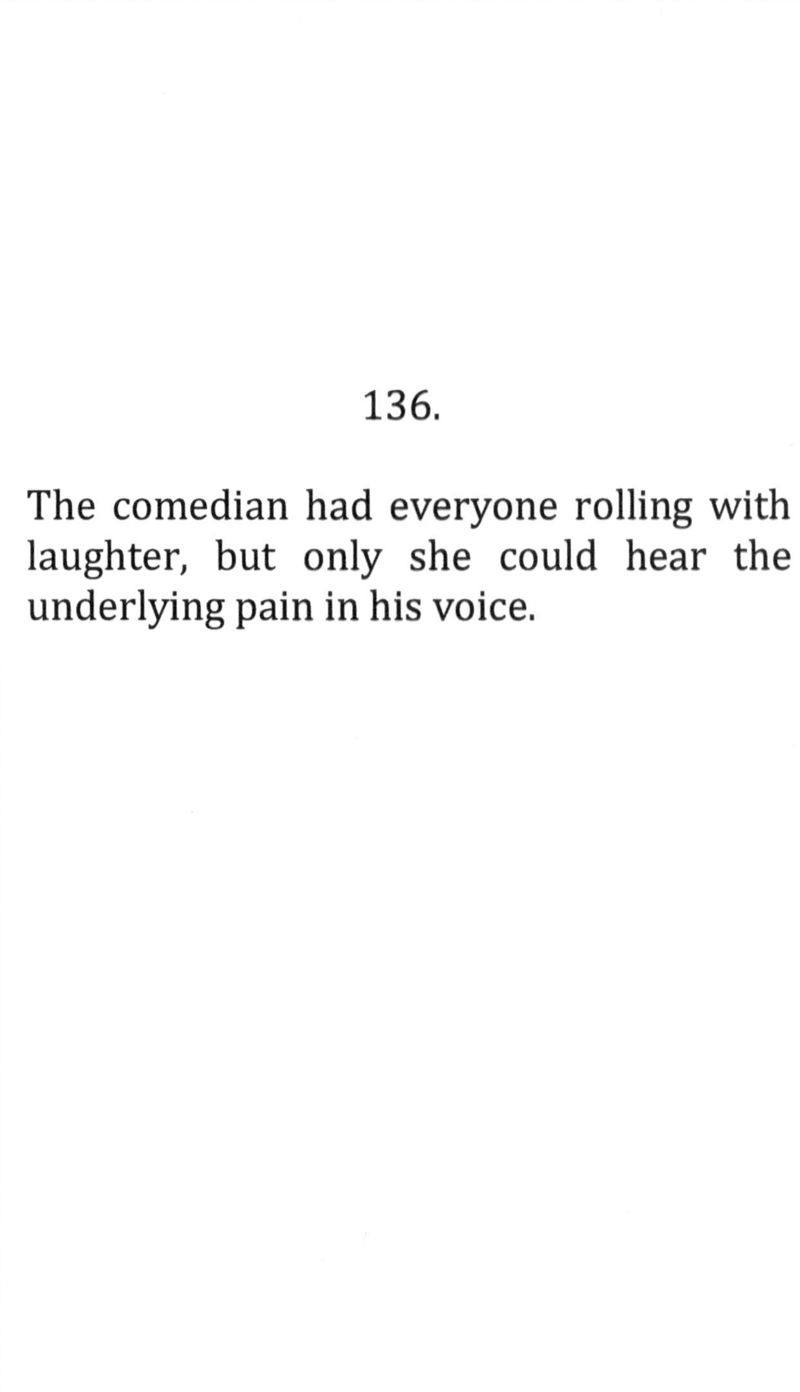

136.

The comedian had everyone rolling with laughter, but only she could hear the underlying pain in his voice.

137.

The looming gloomy clouds and the charcoal night might look sinister, but don't give up...hold on a bit more, for the sun will soon rise sharply and dissipate the darkness with its brilliance.

138.

When life gave me lemons, I offered them to a guy with soda, and here we are today, happily together and effervescent ever since.

139.

The first rays of dawn had never seemed so glorious before. Her new spectacles of hope and optimism were really working.

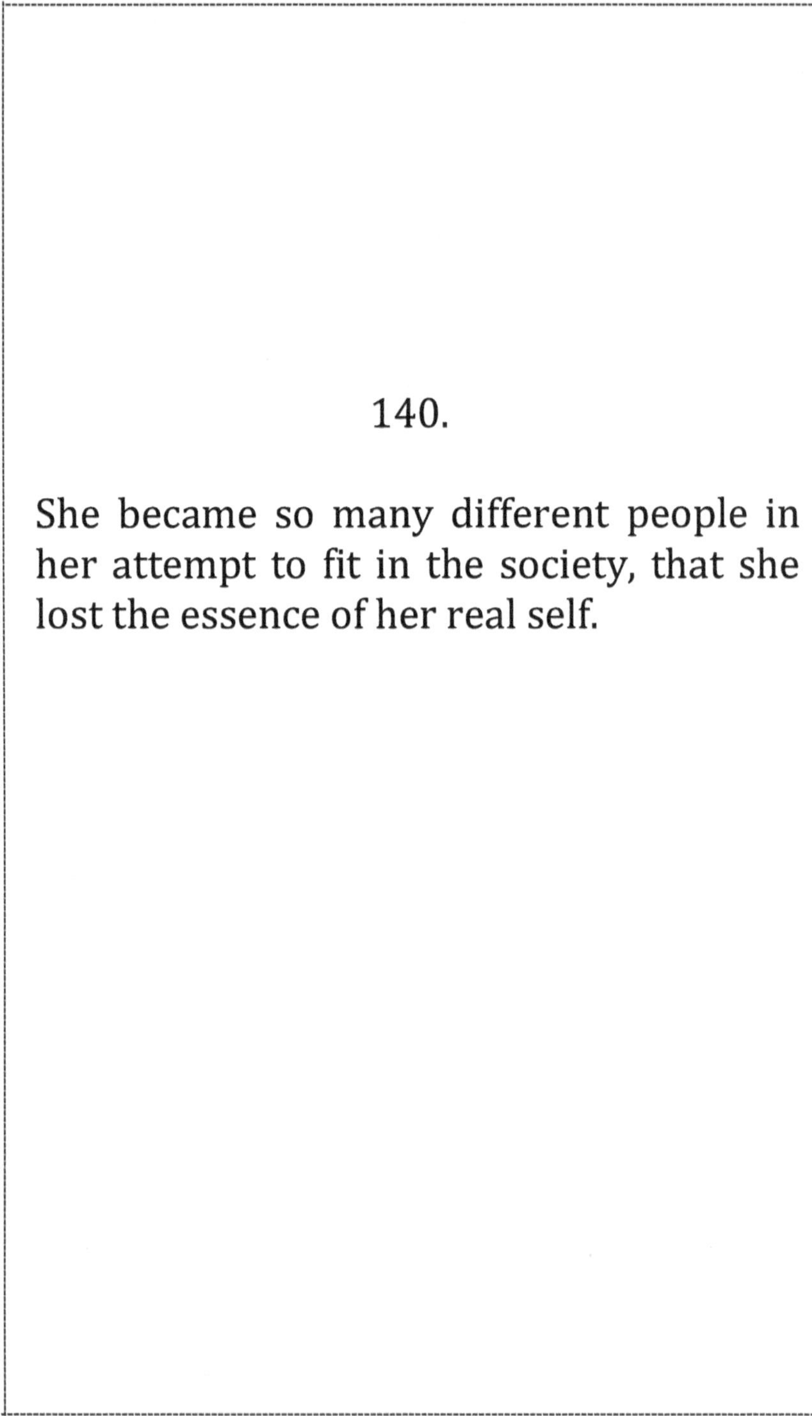

140.

She became so many different people in her attempt to fit in the society, that she lost the essence of her real self.

141.

The mirror knew it all- my pain, failures and weaknesses, but it chose to reflect only my hidden confidence, capability and strength... propelling me towards success.

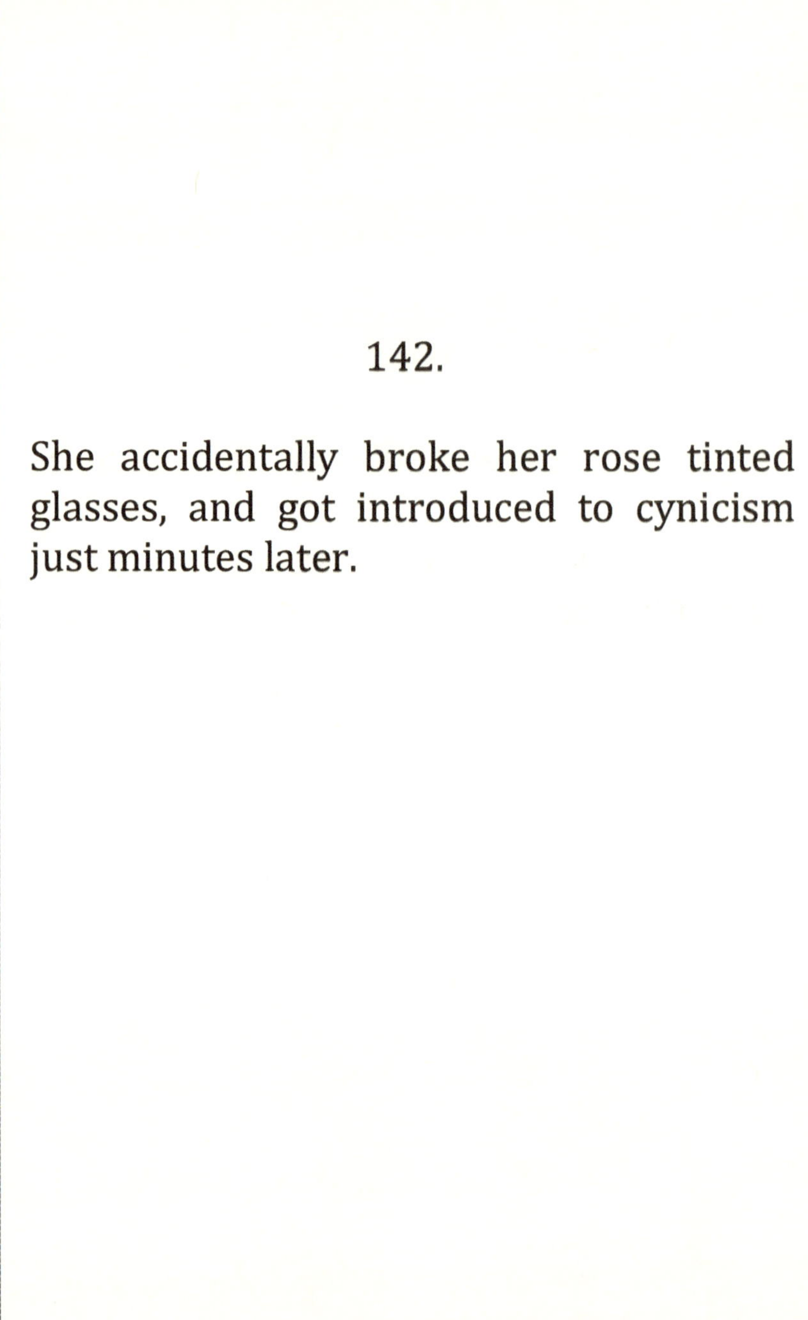

142.

She accidentally broke her rose tinted glasses, and got introduced to cynicism just minutes later.

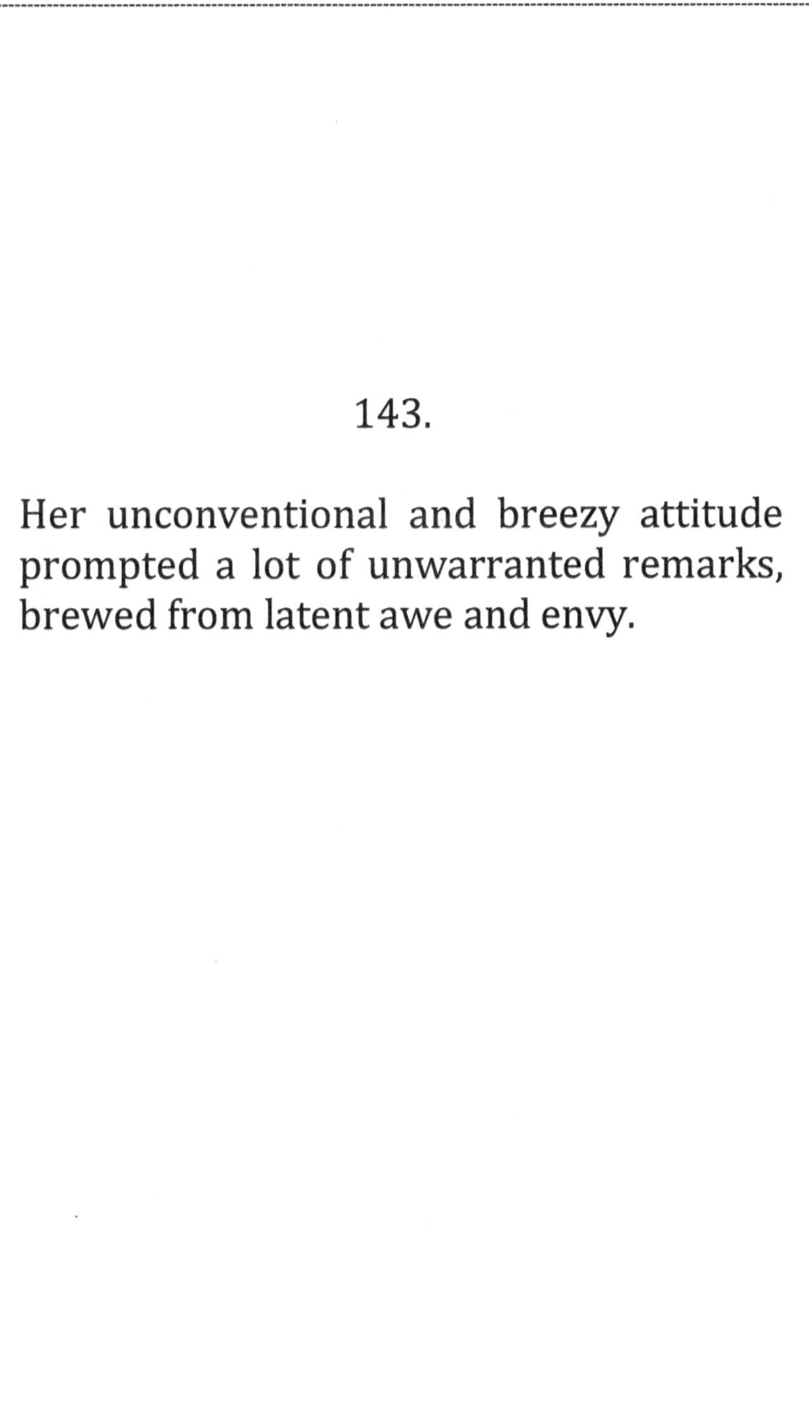

143.

Her unconventional and breezy attitude prompted a lot of unwarranted remarks, brewed from latent awe and envy.

144.

The more you change your colours, the more they reflect in me.

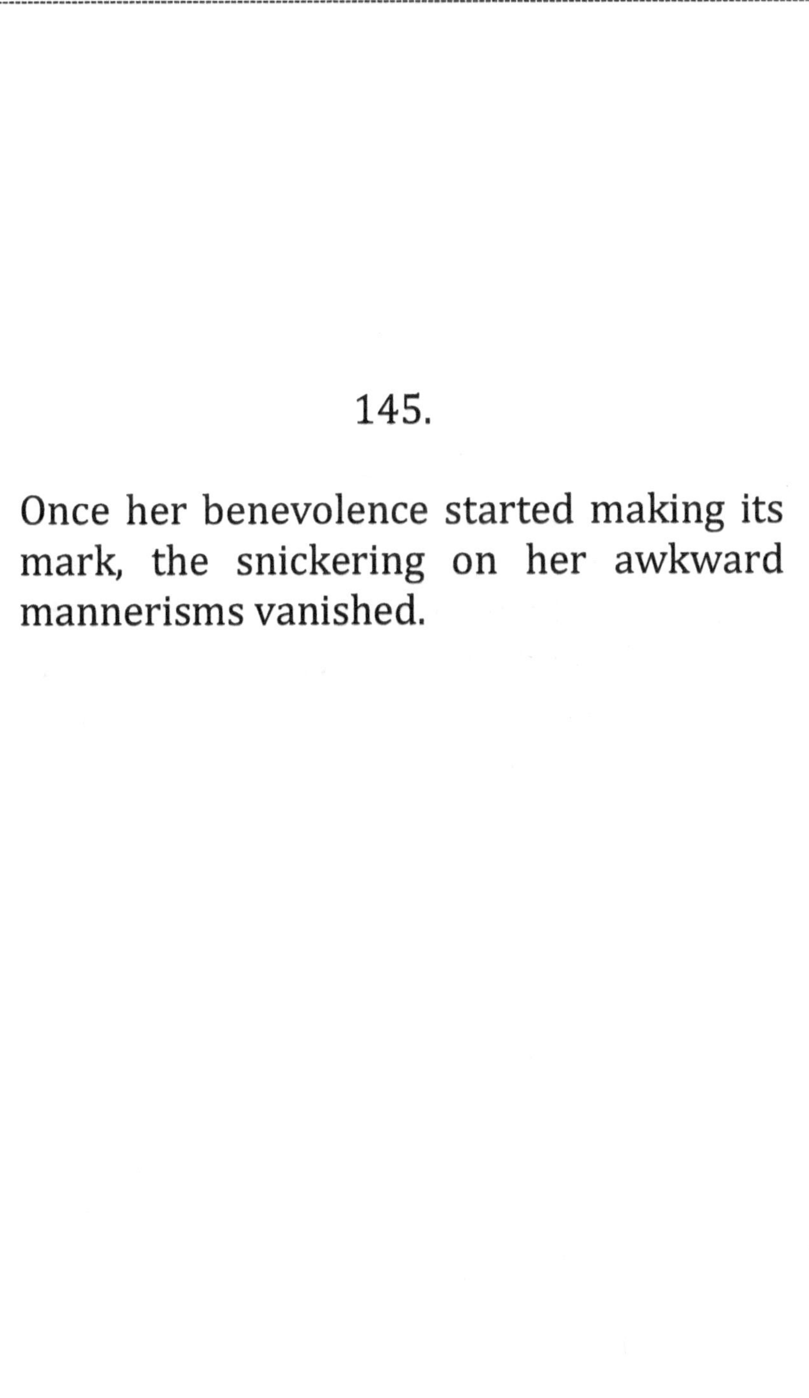

145.

Once her benevolence started making its mark, the snickering on her awkward mannerisms vanished.

146.

"It is not that I don't like people, but the profound silence here makes more sense to me than the incoherent murmurs of the mankind." said a hermit who lived alone in the wilderness.

147.

She was a naive little princess who grew up to learn that life stops being a fairytale at some point, and you have to switch from being a princess to a witch sometimes, if you want to survive sanely in this not so fairytalish world.

148.

The enthralled audience erupted in thunderous applause after her dance performance. Thanking everyone profusely, she rushed to the green room and sat down as tears of joy streamed down her face. "Our perseverance is finally making its mark but don't get conceited, we still have a long way to go." She lovingly said to her prosthetic leg as she took it off.

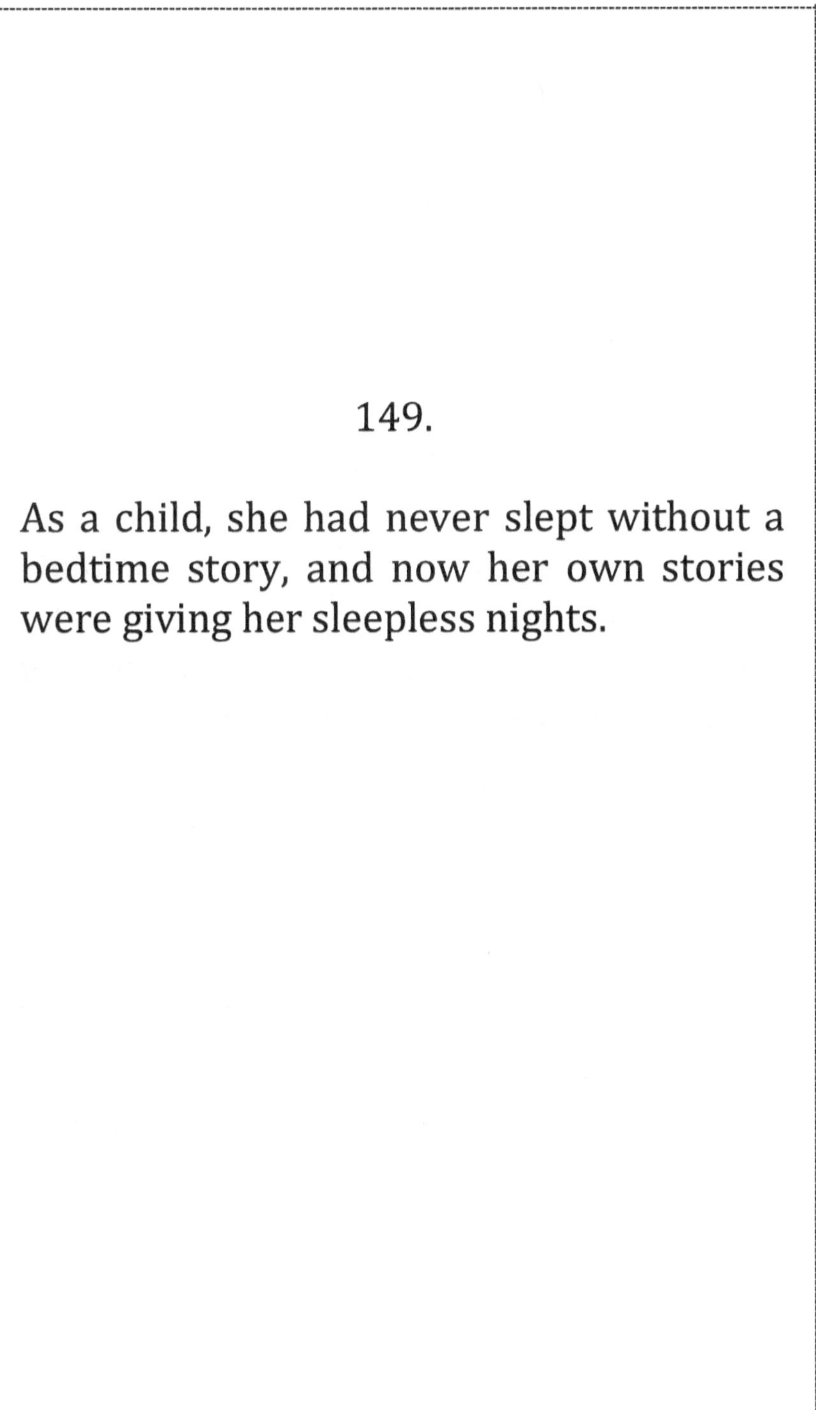# 149.

As a child, she had never slept without a bedtime story, and now her own stories were giving her sleepless nights.

150.

Like every day, he got off his Harley, took off his stylish glares, smoothened his hair spikes and tucked in his shirt before walking towards the temple. The star of the college had his own secret star.

About The Author

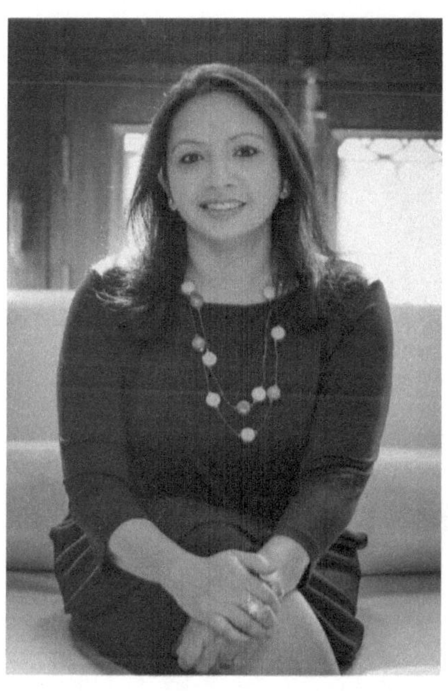

Anjali started her career as a Radio Jockey with Big 92.7 FM. She now runs her own content writing company. Anjali lives in her hometown, the beautiful city of lakes, Udaipur with her husband, daughter and their dog. She has a bachelor's degree in science, master's degree in English literature and a diploma in international business. Although this is her first book, she has been in a steady relationship with writing since long, as she puts it.

Other Titles By Half Baked Beans
Available On Amazon & Flipkart

NAVEENA SRINIVAS
SWETA NAVEEN
GREY TO BLACK

HASHTAG
STORY
GARIMA BATRA
PRARTHANA EARLA

the
GREAT
INDIAN
anthology
EXPRESS EDITION
VOLUME 2

WAITING FOR
TSUNAMI
2040

CODENAME:
SPECTER
KARTHIK C
SHIVAM JAYANT

THE SOUND
OF BOOTS
MERENA TOPPO
MANSI SHARMA
NIVEDITA A
DIKSHITA SAIKIA

NEVERFOUND
LAND
DURRIYA
KAPASI

WILD
CARD 3
never say never
ASFIYA RAHMAN

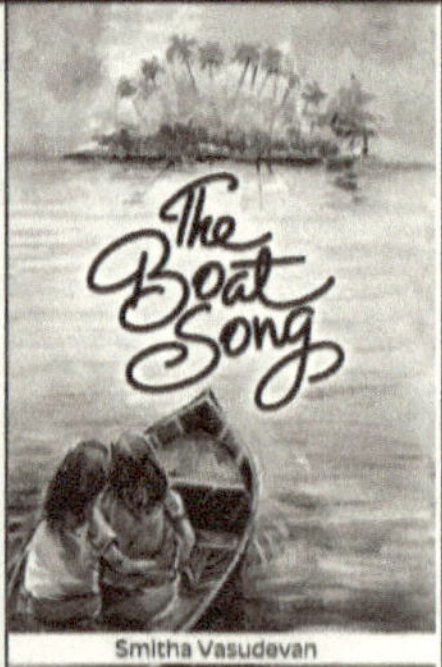

The
Boat
Song
Smitha Vasudevan

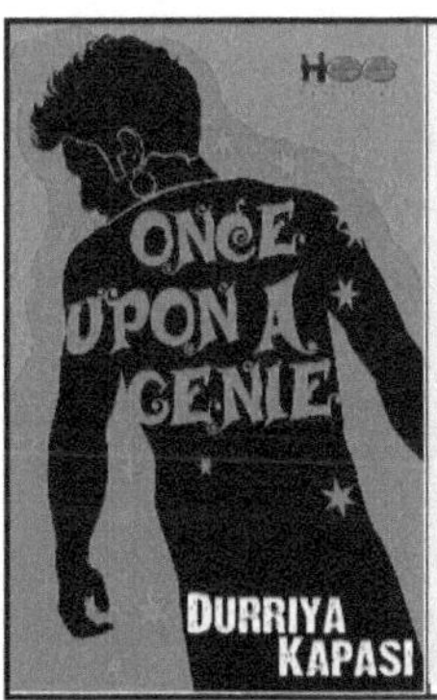
ONCE UPON A GENIE
DURRIYA KAPASI

a fallen leaf
a collection of short stories
produced by
penmancy writers

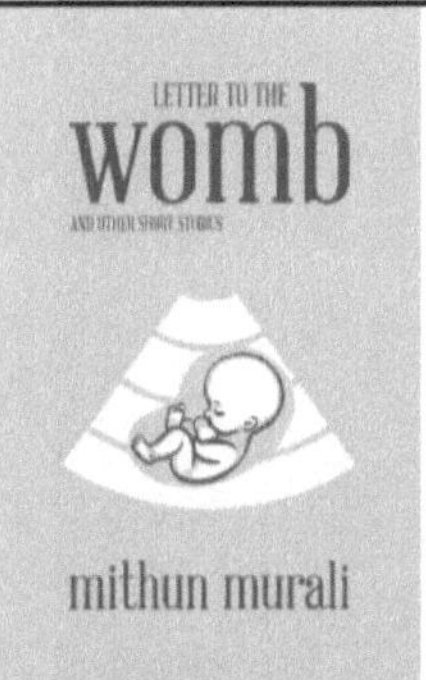
LETTER TO THE
womb
AND OTHER SHORT STORIES
mithun murali

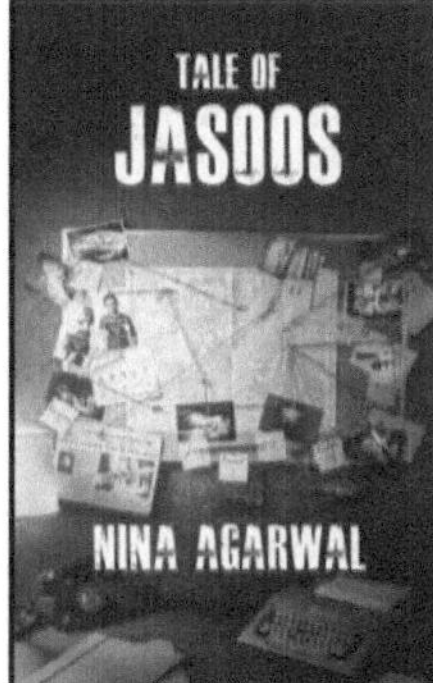
TALE OF
JASOOS
NINA AGARWAL

the
GREAT
INDIAN
anthology
VOLUME 1
An initiative by
H

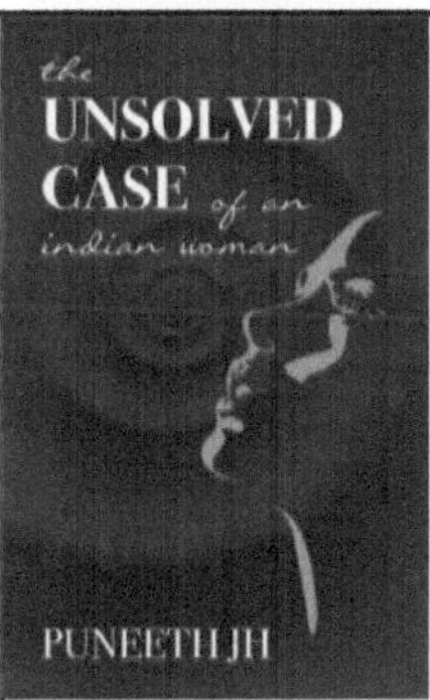
the
UNSOLVED
CASE of an
indian woman
PUNEETH JH

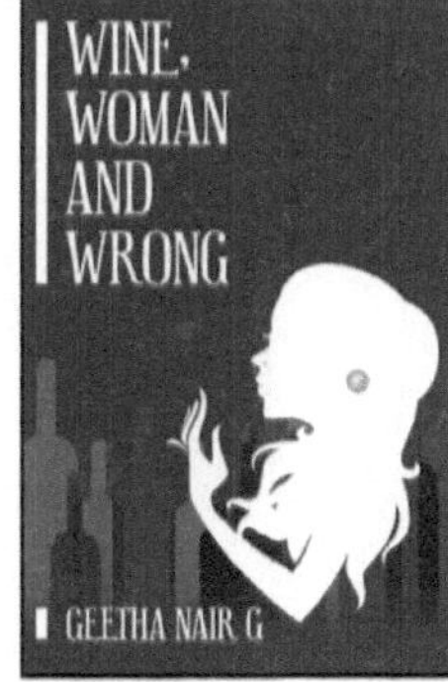
WINE,
WOMAN
AND
WRONG
GEETHA NAIR G

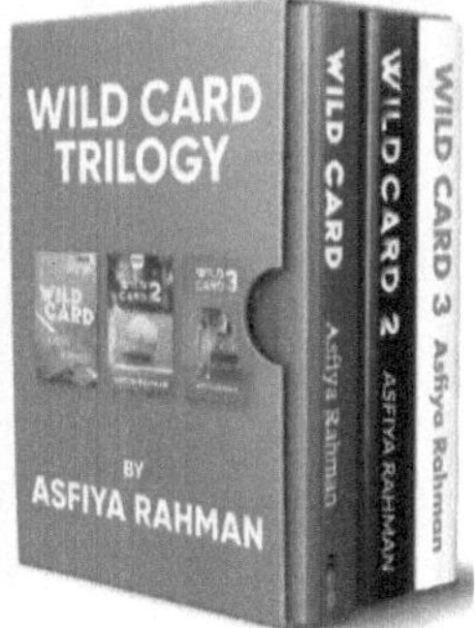
WILD CARD
TRILOGY
BY
ASFIYA RAHMAN
WILD CARD
WILD CARD 2 Asfiya Rahman
WILD CARD 3 Asfiya Rahman

www.ingramcontent.com/pod-product-compliance
Lightning Source LLC
Chambersburg PA
CBHW031313160726
47993CB00001B/404